Hello everyone,

It's Santa here! Christmas is coming and I'm sure you're all very excited. Now it's time to send me your very own letter with your Christmas wishes.

You can use the writing paper from inside the big envelope.

Don't forget to write my address on the envelope and add one of my special sticker stamps:

Santa Claus
Santa's Grotto
North Pole

Post your letter soon so that I can get your presents ready in time!

Merry Christmas!

Santa Claus
xx

Ho, ho, ho!

To Lynn, with love
~ K W

For my Ema and Mima
~ P L

LITTLE TIGER PRESS
1 The Coda Centre, 189 Munster Road,
London SW6 6AW
www.littletiger.co.uk

First published in Great Britain 2012

A CIP catalogue record for this book is
available from the British Library

Printed in China • LTP/1400/1575/0616

2 4 6 8 10 9 7 5 3 1

Dear Santa

Kathryn White   Polona Lovsin

LITTLE TIGER PRESS
London

Little Bear was playing in the snow when
a gust of wind blew a letter past him. As he
picked it up he squeaked in surprise.

"It's a letter for Santa!" he cried. "Oh no!
It must have got lost. If Santa doesn't get this then
somebody won't have their Christmas present!"
So he ran off to see if Rabbit could help.

"Rabbit!" called Little Bear, racing up
the path. "I've found a letter for Santa.
We must take it to him!"

"Tails and whiskers!" cried Rabbit.
"How exciting!"

"Ooh – I love an adventure!" smiled
Little Bear, as they rushed around,
packing some scrumptious snacks.

"This way!" said Rabbit and they
marched through the crunchy
snow in the wintry sunshine.
They walked over hills and
down long, country lanes until at last
they reached the sparkling sea.

Rabbit held on tight as Little Bear paddled their tiny boat out across the waves. They bobbed up and down, all the way out to sea.

"Look!" cried Rabbit. "Penguins! Hello, Penguins! Do you know the way to Santa's grotto?"

The penguins waved cheerily. "It's up the big mountain," they called. "Good luck!"

And Little Bear and Rabbit paddled on towards the shore.

The friends climbed up the steep mountain, higher
and higher. Snow began to fall, and the wind howled.

"Which way now?" called Little Bear.

"Just follow that path," came a friendly hoot.

"Thank you, Mr Owl!" said Rabbit.

Little Bear and Rabbit trudged along, but it
was growing dark and cold. Soon the path
was hidden beneath the falling snow.

"Oh no! I think we're lost," cried Rabbit.

"We'll never reach Santa in time," said Little Bear sadly.

"Did you say Santa?" said a reindeer, trotting up. "I'm going to Santa's grotto. Hop on!"

Little Bear and Rabbit giggled as they soared across the starry sky.

"It's beautiful," whispered Little Bear.

When at last Reindeer landed, they were right outside the twinkly lights of Santa's grotto!

Little Bear and Rabbit rushed in.

  "Santa!" they cheered and raced up
to show him the letter.

  "What do we have here?" said Santa kindly.
"You've brought a letter all this way? What
brave adventurers you are."

Santa opened the envelope and
slowly read the letter.

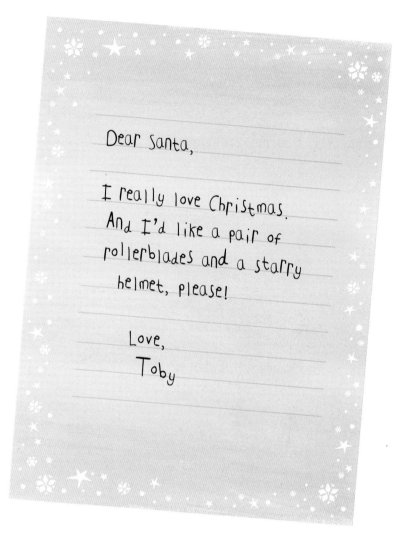

Dear Santa,

I really love Christmas.
And I'd like a pair of
rollerblades and a starry
helmet, please!

Love,
Toby

"Well, we'd better get on to it!"
Santa chuckled. "Would you like to
help my mice make the presents?"

"Oooh yes!" cried Little Bear
and Rabbit.

Santa's workshop was full of wonderful toys. Mice scurried about, painting and wrapping presents.

Soon Toby's rollerblades and starry helmet were ready.

"This is such fun!" laughed Rabbit,
helping Little Bear tie the ribbon.

Santa loaded the sleigh with all the gifts and soon
they were flying high above the snowy rooftops.

"Hold on tight!" Santa shouted.

Little Bear and Rabbit watched as Santa
whizzed down chimneys, delivering presents
to all the boys and girls.

When the sleigh arrived at Toby's house, Santa put his hat on Little Bear's head.

"I think you should deliver this," he said.

Little Bear was so excited. He tiptoed in and carefully placed Toby's present under the shimmering Christmas tree.

"Well done, you two!" said Santa. "You've made Toby's Christmas very special indeed." Little Bear and Rabbit smiled proudly, as Santa gave them each a special gift.

"Happy Christmas,"
Santa cheered and
he sped away in his
twinkly sleigh.

When Little Bear woke up on Christmas morning he raced round to Rabbit's house.

The two friends played with their new toys and talked about their big adventure.

"This has been the best Christmas ever!" Little Bear smiled and he gave Rabbit a happy Christmas hug.